Mr. Putter and Tabby
Pour the Tea

CYNTHIA RYLANT

Mr. Putter and Tabby
Pour the Tea

Illustrated by
ARTHUR HOWARD

Harcourt Brace & Company

San Diego New York London

For Grandmama and Whiskers
—C. R.

For James Tilton
—A. H.

Text copyright © 1994 by Cynthia Rylant
Illustrations copyright © 1994 by Arthur Howard

Requests for permission to make
copies of any part of the work should be mailed to:
Permissions Department, Harcourt Brace & Company, 6277 Sea Harbor Drive,
Orlando, Florida 32887-6777.

Library of Congress Cataloging-in-Publication Data
Rylant, Cynthia.
Mr. Putter and Tabby pour the tea/Cynthia Rylant;
illustrated by Arthur Howard. — 1st ed.
p.   cm.
Summary: Mr. Putter gets an old cat to share his life with him.
ISBN 0-15-200282-0
[1. Cats — Fiction. 2. Old age — Fiction.] I. Howard, Arthur, ill. II. Title. III. Title:
Mr. Putter and Tabby pour the tea.
PZ7.R982Mt   1994
[E] — dc20   93-21470

Special Edition for Troll Book Fairs

A B C D E

Printed in Singapore

1
Mr. Putter

Before he got his fine cat, Tabby,
Mr. Putter lived all alone.

In the mornings he had no one
to share his English muffins.
In the afternoons he had no one
to share his tea.

And in the evenings there was no one Mr. Putter could tell his stories to. And he had the most wonderful stories to tell.

All day long as Mr. Putter
clipped his roses
and fed his tulips
and watered his trees,
Mr. Putter wished for
some company.

He had warm muffins to eat.

He had good tea to pour.

And he had wonderful stories to tell.

Mr. Putter was tired of living alone.

Mr. Putter wanted a cat.

2

Tabby

Mr. Putter went to the pet store.

"Do you have cats?" he asked the

pet store lady.

"We have fourteen," she said.

Mr. Putter was delighted.

But when he looked into the cage,

he was not.

"These are kittens," he said.

"I was hoping for a cat."

"Oh, no one wants cats, sir,"

said the pet store lady.

"They are not cute.

They are not peppy."

Mr. Putter himself had not
been cute and peppy for a
very long time.
He said, "I want a cat."

"Then go to the shelter, sir,"
said the pet store lady.
"You are sure to find a cat."

Mr. Putter went to the shelter.

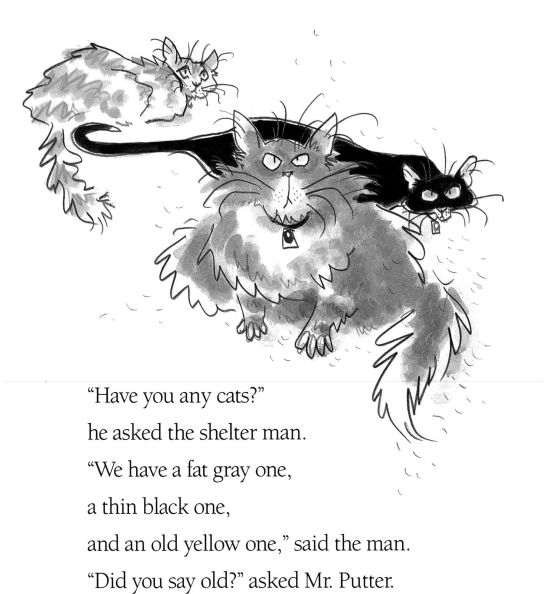

"Have you any cats?"

he asked the shelter man.

"We have a fat gray one,

a thin black one,

and an old yellow one," said the man.

"Did you say old?" asked Mr. Putter.

The shelter man brought Mr. Putter
the old yellow cat.
Its bones creaked,
its fur was thinning,
and it seemed a little deaf.
Mr. Putter creaked,
his hair was thinning,
and he was a little deaf, too.

So he took the old yellow cat home.

He named her Tabby.

And that is how their life began.

3

Mr. Putter and Tabby

Tabby loved Mr. Putter's tulips.
She was old,
and beautiful things
meant more to her.

She would rub past all
the yellow tulips.
Then she would roll past
all the red tulips.

Then she would take her bath
among all the pink tulips.
Mr. Putter clipped roses
while Tabby bathed.

In the mornings

Mr. Putter and Tabby liked to share

an English muffin.

Mr. Putter ate his with jam.

Tabby ate hers with cream cheese.

In the afternoons
Mr. Putter and Tabby
liked to share tea.
Mr. Putter took his with sugar.
Tabby took hers with cream.

And in the evenings
they sat by the window,
and Mr. Putter told stories.
He told the most wonderful stories.
Each story made Tabby purr.

On summer days they warmed their
old bones together in the sun.
On fall days they took
long walks through the trees.
And on winter days they turned
the opera up *very* loud.

After a while it seemed as if
they had always lived together.
Tabby knew just what Mr. Putter
was going to do next.
Mr. Putter knew just where Tabby
was going to sleep next.

In the mornings each looked for
the other as soon as they
opened their eyes.

And at night each looked for
the other as their eyes were closing.
Mr. Putter could not remember
life without Tabby.

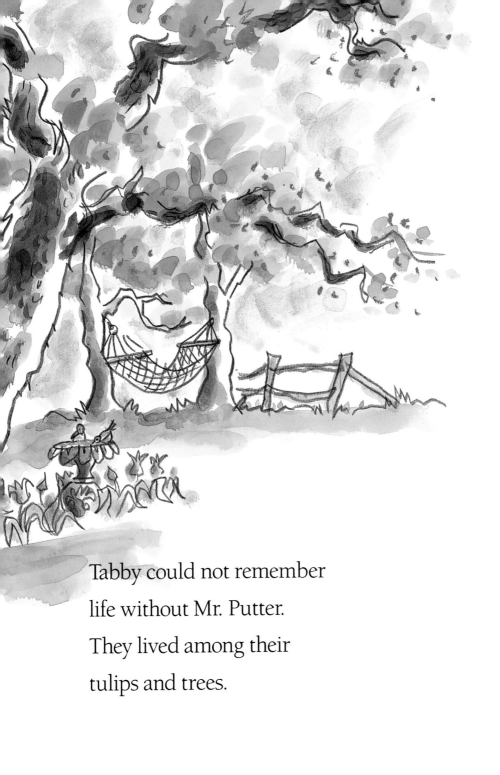

Tabby could not remember
life without Mr. Putter.
They lived among their
tulips and trees.

They ate their muffins.

They poured their tea.

They turned up the opera,

and enjoyed the most

perfect company of all —

each other.

The illustrations in this book were done in pencil, watercolor,
gouache, and Sennelier pastels on 90-pound vellum paper.
The display type was set in Artcraft by Harcourt Brace & Company
Photocomposition Center, San Diego, California.
The text type was set in Berkeley Old Style Book
by Thompson Type, San Diego, California.
Color separations were made by Bright Arts, Ltd., Singapore.
Printed and bound by Tien Wah Press, Singapore
Production supervision by Warren Wallerstein and Ginger Boyer
Designed by Arthur Howard and Trina Stahl